Silly Street

Jeff Foxworthy

Silly Street

Illustrated by Steve Björkman

HarperCollinsPublishers

Silly Street

Printed in the U.S.A.

Library of Congress Cataloging-in-Publication Data is available.
ISBN 978-0-06-171918-9 (trade bdg.) — ISBN 978-0-06-171919-6 (lib. bdg.)

Typography by Rachel Zegar
1 2 3 4 5 6 7 8 9 10
❖
First Edition

To Jordan and Jules:
It is an honor and a joy
being your dad.
—J.F.

For the Hepner family
with great love.
—S.B.

This Way to Silly Street

Sometimes you're silly
And you know that it's true.
When you're feeling that way,
There are things you can do.

Like jumping in circles
Or spinning around.
Try doing cartwheels
Without falling down.

You could stand on your head
And wiggle your toes,
Or just walk around
With a spoon on your nose.

But if you're looking for more
And want something new,
Then I know a cool place
That's just waiting for you.

Silly Street

In the heart of the city
Is a place people meet.
It's this and it's that
And it's called Silly Street.
There are snowballs for sale
If you feel like throwing,
And bubbles to buy
If you feel like blowing.
If you like to jump rope,
There are plenty to use.
There are cots in the shade
If you're needing a snooze.
There are Frisbees to fling
And kites you can fly.
If you like to make noise,
Give the trumpets a try.
There are things you'll see there
You won't see other places,
Like the flying squirrel circus
And pink elephant races.

Snowballs 5¢

Hats and Halos

While on Silly Street
If you yearn for a hat,
You can find what you want
At McDoogle and Pratt.
They have ten thousand hats
And five thousand caps,
Toboggans, tiaras,
Helmets, and wraps.
There are hats for a cowboy
And crowns for a king
And halos for angels
To wear when they sing.

Pets-a-Palooza

Pets-a-Palooza
Is a must stop each visit.
You'll find dogs and fat cats
And "Oh my, what is its?"

Maybe the pet that
you seek is a rabbit.
They don't keep them in cages,
So you'll just have to grab it.

Costumes 'n' More

When was the last time
You dressed like a pig?
Or walked around town
In green pants and a wig?

Sometimes a costume
Can sure make you smile
To pretend to be something
You're not for a while.

You could dress up
Like a pirate or parrot,
Or better yet
As a "thing people stare at."

If this sounds like fun,
Then I know a great store.
It's on Silly Street. Look for
Costumes 'n' More.

The Odds and Ends Market

If you should park at

The Odds and Ends Market,

There's no telling

What you might find:

Square blocks made of wood

And soap that smells good

And boots that are one of a kind.

You can get some of this

And a whole lot of that.

Sometimes it's so hard to decide.

Should you get a big pony

That eats fried baloney

Or a little one that you can ride?

Flo's Flower Shop

If you should stop

At Flo's Flower Shop,

Check out the daisies in back.

See some that are white

And some that are blue

And some that are yellow and black.

Smell orchids and roses.

Just follow your nose as

It takes in the smells that abound.

Find a tub filled with tulips

And pots packed with pansies

And lilies that sell by the pound.

Magic

There used to be a magic store

Run by a man with a beard,

But he pulled out his wand

And gave it a wave

And "poof" the whole store disappeared!

Daffy Dave's Diner

If you get hungry,
And why would you not?
Then Daffy Dave's Diner
Just might hit the spot.
Eat tomatoes, potatoes,
And turkey that's basted.
Mama Mae's meat loaf
Is the best I have tasted.
The waitress is Dottie.
She talks really loud.
Her hair's big and white
And looks like a cloud.
Her husband is Corky.
He works as the cook.
If you don't clean your plate,
He'll give you "the look."

MENU

Turkey
Meat Loaf
Tomatoes
Pota

Diner

House of Clocks

At Mel's House of Clocks
They only sell socks,
Which makes me ask,
"What was Mel thinking?"

He says, "Socks are the thing
That makes the world sing,
'Cause they're warm and keep
Your feet from stinking!"

Phil's Fluffy and Light

At Phil's Giant Pancakes
Business is slow.
They've sold only one
As far as I know.

It was fluffy and light
And the taste! You can't beat it.
But it took four hundred people
A whole year to eat it.

Lost Your Marbles?

If you've lost all your marbles
And need to get more,
I suggest that you try
Mister Mark's Marble Store.

Mark has more marbles
Than you've ever seen
In yellow and orange
And ten shades of green.

Some look like glass
And others like wood.
Buy the glow-in-the-dark kind.
I think that you should.

There are marbles so big.
There are marbles quite small.
Some of them look like
A tiny eyeball.

Feeling Silly

If you're feeling silly,
And you know that you are,
You should buy a balloon
From old Gavin McGarr.

He has some that are long
And some that are round.
There are some you can ride
And fly all over town.

Butterflies

One thing you must see

Is the butterfly tree

Where thousands of butterflies light.

Their wings look like leaves

As they flap in the breeze.

When they leave, it's a rainbow in flight.

Bubble Gum Tree

There used to be a bubble gum tree

On the corner of Silly and White.

But the birds picked it clean,

'Twas a sight to be seen.

There were crows blowing bubbles in flight.

Daily Parade

On Silly Street there's a daily parade.

It begins right in front of Arnie's Arcade.

Ten elephants lead a band of baboons

And the baton-twirling feats of two wacky raccoons.

Watch the craziest clowns

That you've ever seen

With hair red, white, and blue,

Pink, yellow, and green.

A team of six huskies
Pulls a bathtub on wheels.
It holds Tic, Tac, and Toe,
The singing blue seals.

Next it's two giant turtles
Named Ollie and Ned,
With a girl on their backs
With a cat on her head.

Then skunks riding skateboards
And chickens that dance
And a lady on stilts
Wearing verrrrry long pants.

Boo Boo McGrew

Don't be silly; of course there's a petting zoo.
It's run by a farmer named Boo Boo McGrew.
He's got all kinds of animals that you've never seen,
Like a pig that does flips on a green trampoline.

There's a cow that says "quack"; how silly is that?
And a sheep that likes wearing a big birthday hat.
There's a very long dog with a very big smile.
If you scratch his back, it might take quite a while.

Have you ridden an ostrich?
Well, here is your chance.
It's so fun when they run
And they spin and they dance.

Just jump in the saddle
And hold on real tight,
'Cause when they stop really fast
You are bound to take flight.

Sweet Tooth

Bud and Ruth have a booth

Called the Sweet Tooth

Loaded with tons of delights.

Taste taffy that's twirly

Or fudge that is curly

Or my favorite, the berryball bites.

Eat sugar-spun oodles

And gummy yum noodles.

Sometimes it's so hard to decide.

I love coconut clusters

And rainbow jaw busters.

My dentist saw them and he cried.

Merry-Go-Round

In the center of town
There's a merry-go-round,
And I must say
It's the best I have found.

Of course there's a horse,
But there is, oh, so much more.
Hop on Leo the Lion
And let out a roar.

You can ride the blue cow
Or the purple giraffe.
Sit on Zippo the Hippo
And try not to laugh.

The Best Sandbox Ever

Do you like a sandbox?
You know most people do.
Then there's a big treat
Just waiting for you.

It's half a block long
And twenty feet high.
It's the best sandbox ever.
That, you cannot deny.

What is it you'd like
To do with the sand?
You might find a friend
To lend you a hand.

You could make a mountain
And climb to the top.
Oh, the list of the things
You could do doesn't stop.

You could fill up a bucket
And pour it back out.
You could dig a big hole
And fill it with trout.

Perpetual Puddle

If you should stop at Perpetual Puddle,

When you're finished jumping, the water and mud'll

    cover your clothes and be in your hair.

Your mother will scream and people will stare.

Mister Billy

On the street that is Silly

Lives a lady named Tillie.

She has a pet goat

She calls Mister Billy.

Billy is famous for all that he eats.

He'll eat up your socks

And he'll eat pickled beets.

He's eaten my shoes and even a jar.

He once tried to chew up a yellow sports car.

Pigeon Lady

The pigeon lady

Is known as Ms. Snerds.

She sits on a bench

And sings to the birds.

She gives them her popcorn,

Her crackers and bread.

The pigeons adore her.

They sit on her head.

House of Popsicles

There's Gordon McNichols
Who with his wife Pickles
Runs a quaint little shop
Called the House of Popsicles.
They have every flavor
You've ever dreamed of.
There's orange beyond orange
And blueberry true love.
The lemon's so sour
It will cross your eyes
And shrink your brainpower
To one half its size.
Triple cherry's a treat
For the old and the young.
It leaves you with a smile
And a very red tongue.

Pogostick Pete

Pogostick Pete
Never stops hopping.
He hops while he's shaving
And hops when he's shopping.
He hops when he's happy.
He hops when he's blue.
And if you get in his way,
He'll just hop over you.

The Biggest Tree House

On the side of the street
In a fabulous tree
Is the biggest tree house
You ever will see.

You are welcome to climb
Clear up to the sky.
Wave the flag at the top
'Cause you're higher than high.

You could meet with your club,
Yell hello to your friends,
'Cause in the great tree house
The fun never ends.

You can wave to the birds,
You can sing really loud,
And on the right day
You can hide in a cloud.

Silly Street, Again

At the end of the day,

At the end of the street,

You're sure to be smiling.

You're sure to be beat.

And you'll know in your heart

If it's sunny or chilly,

There's a place you can go

If you need to be silly.